Saxophone Duets

Seven attractive pieces
arranged by Keith Stent
for two Altos or
Alto & Tenor with piano

Kevin Mayhew

We hope you enjoy *Saxophone Duets*
Further copies of this and other enjoyable collections
are available from your local music shop.

In case of difficulty, please contact the publisher direct:

The Sales Department
KEVIN MAYHEW LTD
Rattlesden
Bury St Edmunds
Suffolk IP30 0SZ

Phone 01449 737978
Fax 01449 737834

Front Cover: *The Lovers' Picnic* by Auguste Hadamard (1823-1886).
Reproduced by courtesy of Fine Art Photographic Library, London.

Cover designed by Graham Johnstone and Veronica Ward

First published in Great Britain in 1996 by Kevin Mayhew Ltd.

ISBN 0 86209 723 1
Catalogue No: 3611180

The music in this book has been arranged by
Keith Stent and is the copyright of Kevin Mayhew Ltd.

Music Editors: Rosalind Dean and Donald Thomson
Music Setting: Tracy Cracknell

Printed and bound in Great Britain by Caligraving Limited, Thetford, Norfolk

Contents

KEITH STENT, who selected and arranged the music in this book, is a conductor at Trinity College of Music in London, where he was formerly a Professor. He also served for twelve years as Chief Examiner for the College's worldwide external examinations.

He has conducted many music societies and windbands, and is a busy consultant, adjudicator and performance coach.

THE GENDARMES' DUET

Jacques Offenbach (1819-1880)

PASTORAL SYMPHONY from 'Messiah'

George Frideric Handel (1685-1759)

THINGS ARE SELDOM WHAT THEY SEEM
from 'HMS Pinafore'

Arthur Sullivan (1842-1900)

16

Saxophone Duets

*Seven attractive pieces
arranged by Keith Stent
for two Altos or
Alto & Tenor with piano*

II ALTO SAXOPHONE

Kevin
Mayhew

THE GENDARMES' DUET

Jacques Offenbach (1819-1880)

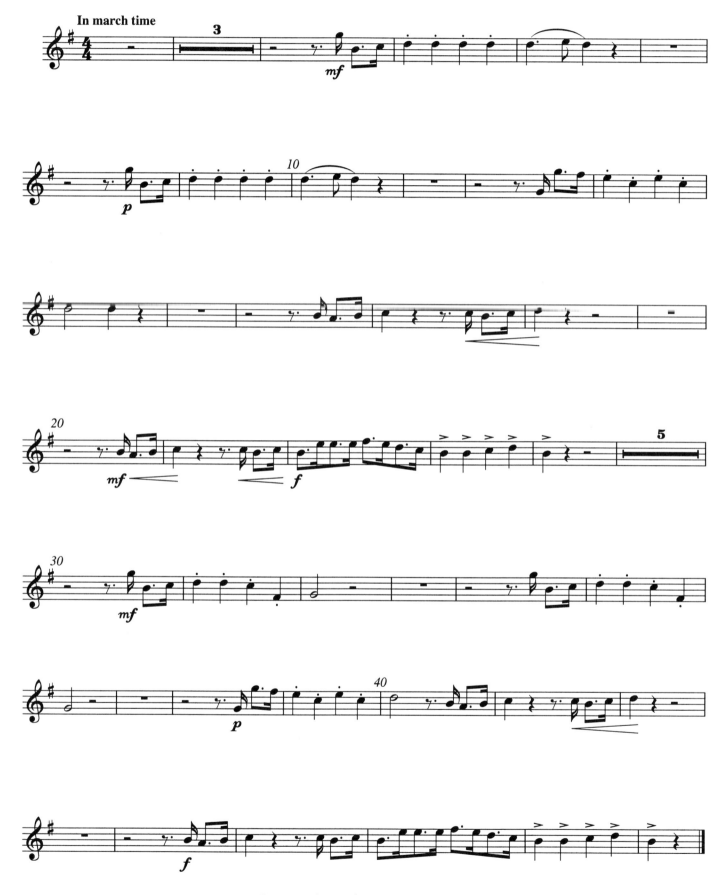

PASTORAL SYMPHONY from 'Messiah'

George Frideric Handel (1685-1759)

THINGS ARE SELDOM WHAT THEY SEEM
from 'HMS Pinafore'

Arthur Sullivan (1842-1900)

PRIESTS' DUET from 'The Magic Flute'

Wolfgang Amadeus Mozart (1756-1791)

BARCAROLLE from 'The Tales of Hoffman'

Jacques Offenbach (1819-1880)

NONE SHALL PART US from 'Iolanthe'

Arthur Sullivan (1842-1900)

CHILDREN'S MARCH

Franz Schubert (1797-1828)

Saxophone Duets

Seven attractive pieces
arranged by Keith Stent
for two Altos or
Alto & Tenor with piano

I ALTO SAXOPHONE

Kevin
Mayhew

THE GENDARMES' DUET

Jacques Offenbach (1819-1880)

2

PASTORAL SYMPHONY from 'Messiah'

George Frideric Handel (1685-1759)

THINGS ARE SELDOM WHAT THEY SEEM
from 'HMS Pinafore'

Arthur Sullivan (1842-1900)

4

PRIESTS' DUET from 'The Magic Flute'

Wolfgang Amadeus Mozart (1756-1791)

BARCAROLLE from 'The Tales of Hoffman'

Jacques Offenbach (1819-1880)

NONE SHALL PART US from 'Iolanthe'

Arthur Sullivan (1842-1900)

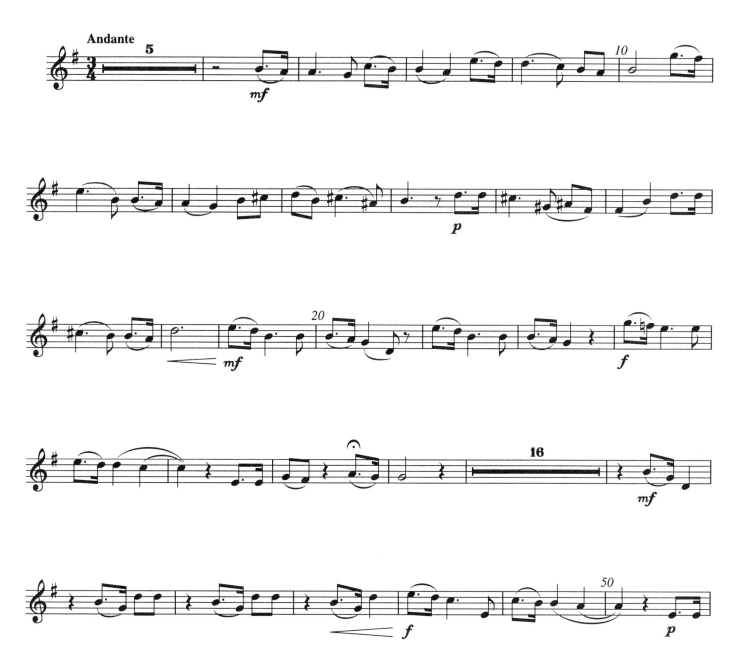

CHILDREN'S MARCH

Franz Schubert (1797-1828)

Saxophone Duets

*Seven attractive pieces
arranged by Keith Stent
for two Altos or
Alto & Tenor with piano*

II Tenor Saxophone

THE GENDARMES' DUET

Jacques Offenbach (1819-1880)

PASTORAL SYMPHONY from 'Messiah'

George Frideric Handel (1685-1759)

THINGS ARE SELDOM WHAT THEY SEEM
from 'HMS Pinafore'

Arthur Sullivan (1842-1900)

PRIESTS' DUET from 'The Magic Flute'

Wolfgang Amadeus Mozart (1756-1791)

BARCAROLLE from 'The Tales of Hoffman'

Jacques Offenbach (1819-1880)

NONE SHALL PART US from 'Iolanthe'

Arthur Sullivan (1842-1900)

CHILDREN'S MARCH

Franz Schubert (1797-1828)

PRIESTS' DUET from 'The Magic Flute'

Wolfgang Amadeus Mozart (1756-1791)

BARCAROLLE from 'The Tales Of Hoffman'

Jacques Offenbach (1819-1880)

NONE SHALL PART US from 'Iolanthe'

Arthur Sullivan (1842-1900)

25

28

CHILDREN'S MARCH

Franz Schubert (1797-1828)

D.C. al Fine

D.C. al Fine